DARK CLAW

for Magnus

May the Guiding Paw be with you

Shoo Rayner

First published in Great Britain in 2002
by Hodder Children's Books

A Catalogue record for this book is available from the British Library

ISBN 978-1-908944-17-7

Tunnel Mazers
Book One

"Now!" hissed Dark Claw.

The Dark Moon control room sprang to life.

Lights flashed. Screens lit up. Somewhere on the secret space station an awesome weapon prepared to fire. Dark Claw smiled an evil smile.

Nearby, a passing Muss spaceship came under attack.

"Help! Our Nosar circuits have blown!" screamed the Muss Captain. "The ship is out of control-o-o-o-o-o-l!"

The small craft hurtled towards the Great Black Hole, and was never seen again.

There is nothing in the known universe that stinks like Fworgonzola. Dark Claw owned the biggest piece of Fworgonzola ever known. He had used it to build his deadly Stonker Ray.

The Stonker Ray could destroy the sensitive Muss Nosar systems, causing chaos for Muss spaceships everywhere.

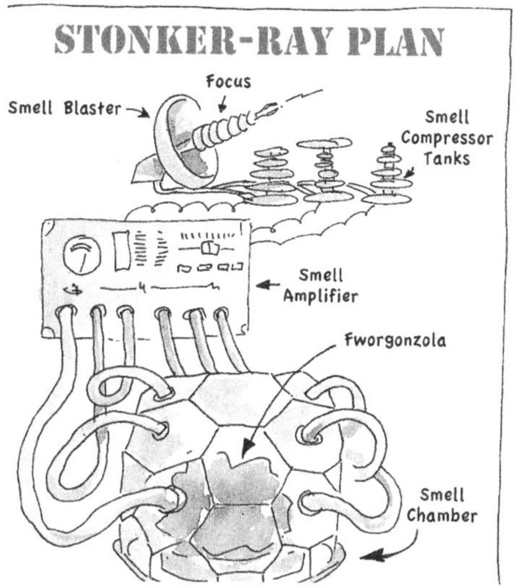

Without their Nosar systems, the Muss could never find their way through the endless distances of space.

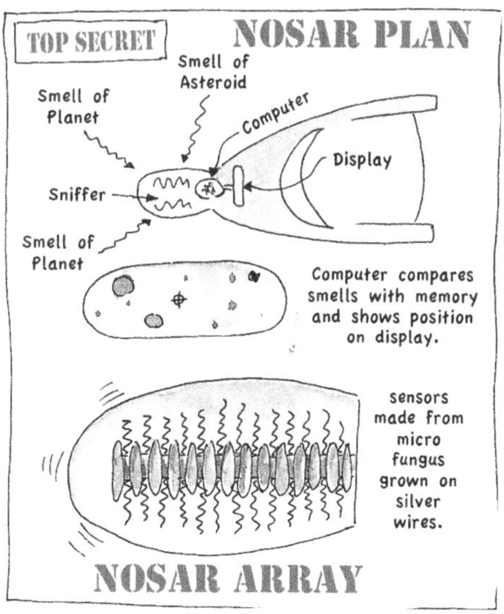

This was just the beginning of Dark Claw's master plan.

He was determined to rid the Universe of Muss forever!

First he sent out a squadron of robot Seekahs to gather information on his enemy. (Kats like to play with their victims first!)

One of the Seekahs flew across the Muss desert towards the Tan Monastery School for gifted young Muss.

The Seekah swept up to the isolated building and hovered silently by a window. Inside, three young Muss were deep in conversation.

"I wish we could win the Tunnel Mazing Cup," said Hammee, the one with glasses. "The first prize is going to be a huge cheddar cheese."

Onlee One, the one with sticking-up hair, sighed. "If odely I was bord wid a sedse of sbell," he said. "Thed our teab bight win for a change."

"Never mind," said Chin Chee, the one with the hair band. "You can't be the best at *everything!*"

The Seekah flew off. But we shall stay with these three young Muss.

*****

Later, at tunnel-mazing practice, the games teacher, Father Dug, gave his Muss pupils their instructions.

“There are two ways out today,” he explained.” One exit has a Cheddar cheese smell and the other smells of Red Leicester. These smells are very similar. It’ll be tricky, but good practice for the finals at the end of term. The first team to come out at the Cheddar cheese hole wins.”

Hammee squeaked, “Can we eat it if we win, sir?”

We’ll see. Father Dug smiled. Hammee was always hungry.

Thirty young Muss poured into the dark tunnels. Sniffing like mad, they searched for the cheesy smells that would lead them to the right exit.

"Phwoor!" someone called out in the darkness. "I can smell Tansy's feet!"

Our trio made a good team. Chin Chee was an excellent smeller. Hammee could find food a hundred miles away, and Onlee One had a razor-sharp photographic memory.

Along the way, he drew a map of the tunnels in his head. If only he could smell as well, he'd be world champion.

"Dare it is!" said Onlee One. "Quig!" He'd spotted the faint glow of light from the exit.

They scrambled out of the hole, but Amber's team had beaten them to it. They were already outside.

Amber sneered and waved the pieces of cheese. "Hey Hammee, look what we've got!"

Hammee was livid. "They always win. It's so unfair!" he complained.

Onlee One's keen eyes spotted something in the far distance.

"What is that?!" he called out. It was a while before the others saw what he was pointing at. A long, black car swept down the desert road towards them.

"It bust be sub-wun really ib-portant," said Onlee One. "Or sub-wun really fabous!"

The car cruised through the school gates and parked out of sight.
Who could it be?

They were just finishing supper that night, when the cook called out, “Onlee One, the Abbot wants to see you.”

Onlee One’s stomach lurched. What could he have done wrong? Everyone watched and whispered as he made his way out of the dining-room.

The cook knocked on the door of Abbot Grey’s study. Onlee One looked up at the name boards on the wall. They listed all the tunnel-mazing champions for over a hundred years. One name stood out in red paint.

The cook saw what he was looking at and sighed. “Pale One! He was the greatest champion of all.”

Onlee One nodded. He had heard many stories about Pale One. There had never been a tunnel-mazer like him before or since.

The cook winked at him. "If you try hard enough, you could be like him one day."

Onlee One shrugged. "It's dot very likely. We bite share de saymb sir-naymb as be, but he didn't have by doze!"

Just then Abbot Grey opened his door. He smiled when he saw Onlee One's worried face.

"It's all right, my boy," he reassured Onlee One. "You haven't done anything wrong."

"I'd like you to meet two of our old students. I taught them both when they were much younger."

Onlee One gasped. He felt he knew the visitors already. Their pictures were in the papers every day. His stomach gurgled loudly as he was introduced to Top Muss, President of the Planet, and Brandling, the Chancellor!

"I-I-I'b pleased to beet you," he stammered.

Abbot Grey motioned him to sit down, then Top Muss began to tell of the peril faced by every single Muss.

Top Muss told Onlee One about Dark Claw and the Stonker Ray. He showed him a tiny piece of Fworgonzola that was sealed in a plexiglass tube.

"Tiny amounts are used to flavour food," he explained. "But the smell from just this little speck would blast our noses and leave us like you, unable to smell.

Brandling explained their plan. “Our Planet is in great danger. We need a very special and brave young Muss to save us all from certain destruction. Onlee One, we think you are that Muss!”

“Because you have no sense of smell, you may be able to get close to the Stonker Ray and destroy it.
We captured one of Dark Claw’s Seekahs and adapted it to carry a small Muss inside.”

That is how we plan to get you on Dark Moon. It is a very dangerous mission. The whole planet is relying on you.

Onlee One gulped. “Why does this Dark Claw want to destroy us all?”

Top Muss gave a deep sigh. “If only we knew.”

Silence filled the room while Onlee One made up his mind. It was a huge challenge. Onlee One's legs shook just thinking about it. But, deep down, he was thrilled to have been chosen. He took a deep breath.

"I will serve you well, but odely if Habbee and Chin Chee cub with be. I deed a teamb dat I can trust."

Hammee and Chin Chee were sent for and agreed to join Onlee One on his mission.

"If Onlee One gets out alive, he'll need us to rescue him," said Chin Chee.

The Abbot agreed. "Any other questions?" he asked.

Hammee lifted a finger. "Er... Any chance of extra food rations?" he asked.

The three young Muss were taken to a

secret training camp. Chin Chee and Hammee spent hours each day, learning to fly a Whisker 320 Space Scout.

"Whoo-hoo!" Chin Chee whooped. "It's just like being in a video game!" Chin Chee loved every minute of her training.

Hammee made sure there were plenty of food rations hidden around the ship… just in case!

Onlee One was taught to fly the captured Seekah. It was a tight squeeze, and hard to fly smoothly. It took a lot of practice.

Two weeks later, they were fully trained and their ship was zooming towards Dark Claw's hideaway, Dark Moon.

It was cold inside the Seekah. The air-lock doors opened and let Onlee One inside Dark Moon.

He landed the little craft in the shadows, where he hoped no one would see him open the hatch.

A door opened noisily. A Robo Kat stood silhouetted in the doorway. Onlee One froze. Could it see him?

Another dumpy robot rumbled in. The door closed behind it. Onlee One had learned his lessons well. The robot was a standard model:RU12 Utility-Kat.

Remembering his training, Onlee One crept up behind it and pressed two red buttons on its back. The robot froze. Three seconds later, the robot clicked and switched off.

"It worked!" thought Onlec One. "They said by photographic bebbory would cub id handy!"

Onlee One climbed through the hatch in the side of the robot. He looked for the red and white wires. He cut them, stripped them, and twisted them together.

Now he was in inside the robot and in complete control it. He could move around Dark Moon without being noticed.

The door opened for him. The guard turned and stared.

Onlee One heard his heart pounding, but the guard didn't suspected nothing. It stood to attention. "Continue!"

"Phew!" The door closed behind the young Muss. He had passed the first test.

****

The other robots ignored Onlee One, as he steered the robot along Dark Moon's corridors. He tried all the doors to see what was behind them.

All the time he drew a map of Dark Moon in his head. If the mission was successful he'd know how to get back to his Seekah and escape.

On level three, he struck lucky. Two guards stood outside a door. Onlee One swept inside and the door closed behind him with a silent swish.

A large machine stood in the middle of the room. It had to be the Stonker Ray.

Onlee One squeezed out of the robot and

took a closer look. Yes! There in the middle of the machine, was a piece of Fworgonzola the size of a ting-tong ball!

He studied the control panel. Under one button the sign read, *eject*. He pushed it. The Fworgonzola slid out on a tray. Onlee One picked it up and sniffed.

"Oh! I thingk I cad sbell sum-ting!" he said, surprised.

As he spoke, the door swished open. Onlee One spun round. A tall, hooded figure stood before him. Yellow eyes glowed with rage.

"GUARDS!"
Boomed Dark Claw.
"Seize him!"

Robo Kats filled the room. Onlee One looked for an escape. The door was the only way out. It was blocked!

There was only one thing for it: *EAT THE FWORGONZOLA!*

He popped it into his mouth and swallowed hard. Yuck! It tasted like old shoe leather!

Dark Claw gasped, "I'll never find so much Fworgonzola again!"

The Robo Kats tried to grab Onlee One.

A bright light burst inside Onlee One's head and he sneezed so loud he nearly turned himself inside out!

The Robo Kats were confused. They turned to Dark Claw for instructions.

Onlee One sniffed. Then he sniffed again. He laughed out loud. "I can smell!"

The Robo Kats' paws couldn't hold him tight enough. Onlee One wriggled from their grasp and dived for the door, but not before Dark Claw lashed at him.

Onlee One felt warm blood trickle down his arm!

Onlee One felt bold and fearless! He ran and ran, somersaulting over Robo Kats. None of them could catch him.

The map in his head was clear as day. He came to the passage where the Robo Kat stood guard over the air-lock hangar door.

"Hey, Metal Boy, over here!" Onlee One taunted.

The young Muss ran at the Robo Kat. He threw himself on the floor and slid right between its legs. He was through the door in no time.

Inside the hangar, he pressed the button to open the air-lock and squeezed inside the Seekah. The Seekah's hatch sealed just in time. Dark Moon's air-lock doors opened and the vacuum of space sucked Onlee One out of the hangar bay and into the vast darkness of space.

He hit a switch to start the radio signal his friends were waiting for. In ten minutes, Chin Chee and Hammee caught him in a net and pulled him to the safety of their ship.

A week later, Hammee and Chin Chee held the huge Cheddar cheese high above their heads and danced.

The annual school tunnel-mazing final had been a walkover. With Onlee One's fantastic new sense of smell, the trio smashed all the school records!

Chancellor Brandling was the guest of honour. She leaned close and spoke quietly to Onlee One as she gave him his prize.

"That's two remarkable performances, young One! I'm sorry we have to keep the first one a secret. Every living Muss owes you a great debt. If only they knew. I hope you feel this cup is a worthy consolation?"

Onlee One took the cup from her. It was a simple design, but it meant more to him than Brandling could ever imagine. The names of all the winners were engraved on the side.

Onlee One was so proud. He fought down the tears. "It's a great honour to follow in the footsteps of great tunnel-mazers like Pale One." He said.

The crowd picked him up and carried him on their shoulders, cheering and clapping their new Champion.

Brandling watched the scene from the edge of the crowd.

"I'm sure we will meet again, young One," she whispered to herself.

Meanwhile, on Dark Moon,
Dark Claw raged.

"Revenge!" he howled.
"I will have my revenge!"

Road Ragers

Book Two

"Woooosh!" Rocket engines screamed. The spaceliner rattled and shook. For three minutes it was hard to move or breathe, but as they headed deep into space, the passengers began to relax.

Onlee One, Chin Chee and Hammee were on their way to the Tunnel-Mazing championships in Muss Vegas on the planet Dice.

The three friends made a brilliant team. They'd been allowed to compete, even though they were still at school.

Hammee spoke with a mouth full of peanuts. “I still can’t believe we’re really going to the Championships.”

Chin Chee laughed. “We wouldn’t be going at all, if Onlee One hadn’t eaten Dark Claw’s piece of Fworgonzola cheese.”

Onlee One smiled and thought to himself. “If I hadn’t eaten it, none of us would be here at all!”

Onlee One had eaten the rare, and very smelly Fworgonzola, and had gained an incredible sense of smell. This had ruined the evil Dark Claw’s deadly plan to destroy the whole of the Muss race. Onlee One shuddered. Dark Claw had come so close to destroying them all.

“I wonder what he’s planning now,” he thought as he watched Planet Muss fade into the distance.

In another corner of space, a Pi-rat ship cruised towards the landing bay of Dark Claw's secret base, Dark Moon. Dark Claw smiled to himself. "At last, they are here."

Dark Claw swept along the corridors to meet the Pi-rat crew in the landing bay.

Their leader was a tall, striking Ratess. She swaggered up to Dark Claw and introduced herself.

"I am Ratuschka. We hear you need some help."

Dark Claw studied her closely. "There's a Muss I need to be rid of," he growled.

Ratuschka's eyes glowed with pleasure.

"Getting rid of Muss is what we do best!"

***

Later, in the control room, they watched secretly filmed video of Onlee One and his friends. Dark Claw pointed at Onlee One.

"He is the special one!" he hissed. "But you can deal with the other two as well."

Dark Claw went through the plan to capture Onlee One.

“Make sure you bring him back alive.” Dark Claw hissed. “I want to watch his final moments!”

Ratuschka smirked. She and her crew were going to enjoy this job. “Leave it to us!” She smirked.

Muss Vegas isn't called "Vacation City" for nothing. It's shiny and glitzy, and all the banners were out for the Inter-Stellar Tunnel-Mazing Championships.

The opening ceremony was spectacular. Chancellor Brandling had come to watch and give the prizes. She spotted Onlee One in the crowd and went to speak with him.

"We meet again, Onlee One!" said the Chancellor. "Good luck, you are playing against the very best now!"

Onlee One's reply was drowned by an incredible noise. The stadium filled with dust.

Throbbing engines announced the entrance of five huge Road Ragers into the stadium. Loud music blared from each of them.

As the sound died away, the drivers climbed out. They were Pi-rats!

Ratuschka waited for the crowd to hush before she spoke. “We wanna play too!”

Rats usually mean trouble, and no one wanted to upset them. But all drivers should have been entered for the competition months before. Brandling took charge and welcomed the newcomers.

“In the spirit of friendship between Muss and Rats, we welcome you and look forward to your good and fair competition.”

Ratuschka met Onlee One’s eyes and smirked. Onlee One shivered and turned to his friends.

“I don’t trust this lot,” he said.

“Good Luck!” Ratushka grinned.

Tunnel-mazing is simple. You go in one hole, go round a maze and come out of another hole. Cheeses are placed at different exit holes. In total darkness, you have to sniff your way to the right exit!

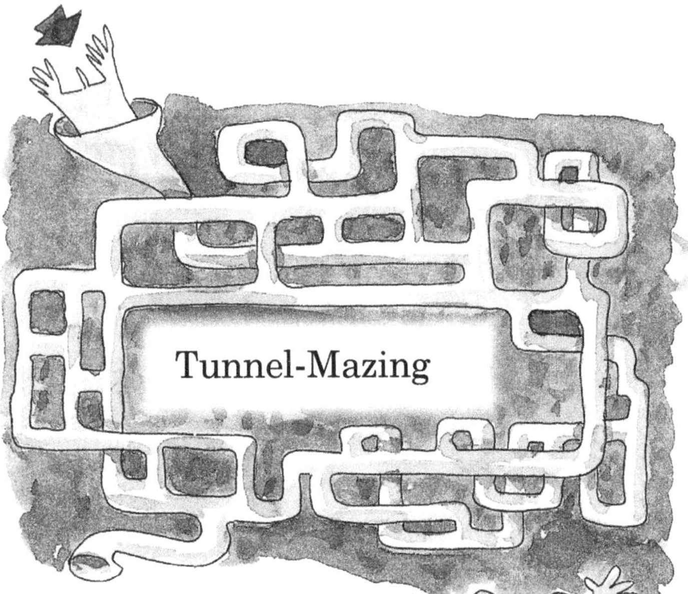

Thanks to the Fworgonzola, Onlee One

now had the best sense of smell of any Muss alive. He also had the ability to draw a map of the maze in his head as he went along.

“Something’s not right,” he whispered to his friends... there’s a new smell.” He sniffed again. “Someone’s dug a new hole since we last came along here.”

A little further on, a shaft of light fell from the roof of the tunnel. “We came down this tunnel five minutes ago,” said Onlee One. “This hole wasn’t here then.”

“Are you sure?” whispered Chin Chee.

“Has he ever been wrong before?“ Hammee tutted.

“Wait here,” said Onlee One. “I’ll see what happens a bit further on.”

Edging forwards into the darkness, his whiskers bristled wildly. Something was very wrong.

He heard a scuffling noise behind him. He turned and ran back the way he had come. His friends had gone… the smell of Rats hung in the air!

Onlee One heard a faint cry. Was it Hammee calling for help?

Onlee One peered out of the hole.

The competition was underway. His team would be disqualified if he left the maze, but that didn't matter now.

Twenty metres away, Hammee and Chin Chee were being bundled into two Road Ragers.

Onlee One scrambled out of the hole, but he was too late. The Road Ragers were already roaring off in a cloud of dust. He would never catch them up.

In the middle of the settling dust, an engine choked. One of the Rats had flooded his engine. He'd have to wait a minute before he could get it started.

The Road Rager was parked next to a flag pole. Onlee One crept up behind it. Without being seen, he let down the flag and used the rope to tie the Road Rager to the pole.

The Rat tried the engine again. It coughed twice, and roared into life. But the wheel was tied and couldn't turn. The inner cockpit, including the driver, turned instead. The Rat spun round fifty times before the engine cut out!

He fell out of his seat and lay on the ground, holding his stomach groaning and retching. He wasn't going anywhere in a hurry - except the toilets!

Quickly, Onlee One untied the rope and climbed into the Road Rager. He talked himself through the controls. "I guess I turn this... and squeeze this... and put my foot down on this...and...woooooah!"

Onlee One soon caught up the other Road Ragers, which were headed straight for a lake. “They’ll have to stop there,” he thought.

But he was wrong. As they hit the water, balloons blew up on the wheels, and they drove right across the lake! At the water’s edge, Onlee One stopped and examined his control panel. He pressed a likely looking button.

Instead of balloons, he was deafened by the loudest music he’d ever heard! The whole machine shook in time with the beat.

Another button had a picture like a wave. Onlee One pressed it…

“Pishhh!”

With a loud woosh, the balloons filled with air and he felt himself lifted on to the surface of the water.

As Onlee One skittered across the surface of the lake, he could see the others in the distance. They had slowed right down, and were circling as if they didn't know which way to go. Then they seemed to make their minds up and zoomed off into the desert.

Onlee One drove up to the same place, stopped, switched off the engine and climbed out.

"Now, why did they stop here?" Onlee One sniffed the breeze. There were two different rat smells in the air.

"Ha!" he laughed out loud. "They've gone the wrong way!"

One rat smell came from the direction the gang had just gone. The other, much fainter smell, led Onlee One to the mouth of a hidden canyon.

A guard lay asleep in the sun. Behind him, in the shadows, was the Pi-rats' spaceship.

Onlee One revved his engine and drove at full speed. His Road Rager roared up the open boarding ramp.

Once inside, he jabbed the ramp shutter button. As the ramp lifted up, he saw the guard running towards the ship, calling out, "Hey, wait for me!"

The inside of the spaceship was a mess.

There was rubbish everywhere. It hadn't been tidied up for years. Onlee One held his nose. "Phew, it stinks!"

He sat in the cockpit and worked out the flight system. Luckily, spaceship controls are pretty much the same wherever you go.

The guard was still banging on the side of the ship as Onlee One started up the engines. Carefully, flying a couple of metres off the ground, he nosed out of the canyon and headed out after the other Road Ragers.

Ratuschka's crew were completely lost and arguing over whose fault it was. "Where's Rabies?" Ratuschka demanded. "He knew the way."

"He was right behind us at the Lake," said Anouschka. "Maybe he's gone to get the ship. Maybe he'll come looking for us."

Nearby, Hammee and Chin Chee were tied to a large rock. Chin Chee listened to the Rats, hoping to find out why they had been taken prisoner.

"I'm hungry!" Hammee whined.

Chin Chee dug her elbow in his ribs.

"You're always hungry... Sshh!"

The Rats began cheering. Chin Chee looked up to see why. The Pi-rat ship was floating across the desert towards them.

Her heart sank. Where would the gang take them to now? The Pi-rats waved and cheered as the first laser blast parted Ratuschka's hair!

They all ducked and the rest of the blasts shot over their heads.

"Hey! Why's he shooting at us?" yelled Ratuschka. "Wait till I get hold of him!"

An echoey voice boomed out of the ship's speaker system.

"If you want this ship back, untie those two and return to Muss Vegas now."

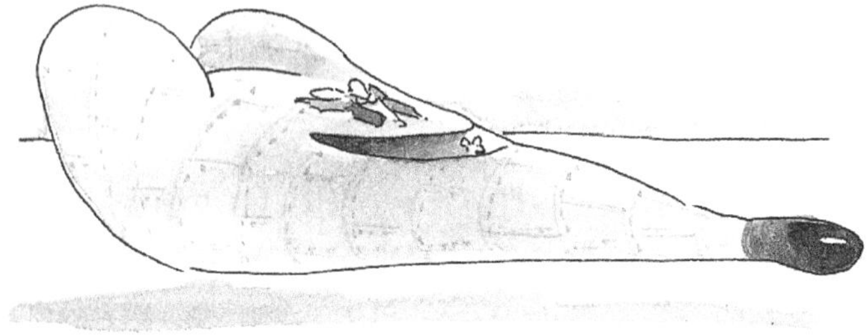

Hammee and Chin Chee cheered. The Pi-rats started arguing again.

"It's Onlee One!"Ratushka screamed at Rattoo. "This is all your fault!"

"I didn't do nuffin!" Ratoo yelled back.

The voice from the ship called again. "You have ten seconds until I start firing again!"

Ratuschka stood up with her paws in the air. "OK! OK!" she shouted.

Climbing into her Road Rager, she spat orders at her crew. "Untie those two and let's get out of here!"

"Phew! That was close."said Chin Chee. The three friends were together again in the Pi-rat ship. Chin Chee told Onlee One what she had heard.

"The Pi-rats are working for Dark Claw. They took us as hostages to make you go back to Dark Moon to save us. I hate to think what Dark Claw wants to do to you."

"I know what I'd like to do to him!" said Hammee. He was searching the spaceship's lockers for food. He opened a tin and sniffed it. "Ugh! I'm not eating any of this stuff! It's disgusting."

The other two smiled. The food must have smelled really bad. Hammee would eat almost anything "Let's get back to civilisation!" laughed Onlee One.

As they flew back to Muss Vegas, they saw the Road Ragers down below them.

“We’ll get there before them,” said Onlee One. “We can tell Brandling what happened. She’ll know what to do for the best.”

In the stadium, a huge crowd watched as the Pi-rats returned.

Brandling decided it would be best not to upset the Rats any more. They would only come back and make more trouble.

Brandling gave Ratushka a golden disc. “This transmitter passport will see you safely home,” she explained. “No one will bother you while it’s switched on.”

Ratuschka examined the disc suspiciously. “How do I know you won’t shoot us down as soon as we get away from here?“

Brandling ignored her question. “Give your master this message,” she said, firmly. “If he wishes harm to any Muss, he will answer to me!

Ratuschka and her gang slinked away and climbed aboard their ship.

When their ship was just a tiny dot in the sky, Brandling turned to the crowd.

"Since the Tunnel-Mazing Championships have had to be cancelled," she explained. "I hereby announce the First Annual Road Rage Championship!"

The crowd roared with delight. They were going to get some sporting action after all!

Of course, Onlee One had a head start on the other drivers, as no one else had ever driven a Road Rager before! No one was surprised when Onlee crossed the finish line first.

Brandling placed the medal round his neck and smiled. "It's so nice to be a winner, isn't it?" she said. "Now, smile for the cameras!"

Meanwhile, on Dark Moon, the Pi-rats stood before Dark Claw and hung their heads in shame.

"You fools! You have failed me!" he spat. "Now I will have to think of another way to seek my revenge."

"Sorry, Dark Claw," whined Ratuschka. "We did our best."

She took the golden disc from her pocket and gave it to Dark Claw.

As Ratushka explained how the device worked and repeated Brandling's message, a smile crept over Dark Claw's face. "This will be useful… next time!" He growled to himself.

Rat Trap
Book Three

Dark Claw paced the control room of his secret space station, Dark Moon. He banged the control desk with his fist. "I will have revenge!" he snarled.

The small gang of Pi-rats in front of him cowered in fear.

"You have failed me once," Dark Claw growled at them. "You will not fail me again."

"N-n-n-no! D-d-d-dark Claw," stammered Ratuschka, the Pi-rat leader. Of course not!

Dark Claw's one mission in life was to rid the universe of all living Muss. But there was one Muss he wanted to destroy above all others… Onlee One.

Though he was still at school, Onlee One had already upset Dark Claw's evil plans. Not once, but twice…

This time Dark Claw would see to it that the interfering Muss would be silenced, once and for all. Dark Claw handed something to Ratuschka.

She examined it closely. It was a small, grey box with a stubby funnel on top.

Ratuschka waited for Dark Claw to tell her what it was.

"It's a smell repeater," he explained. "My Robodroids are fitting hundreds of these devices on the surface of Dark Moon." Ratuschka looked confused, so Dark Claw continued.

"Muss use their excellent sense of smell to navigate through space. Their Nosar systems are so sensitive, they can even smell Dark Moon."

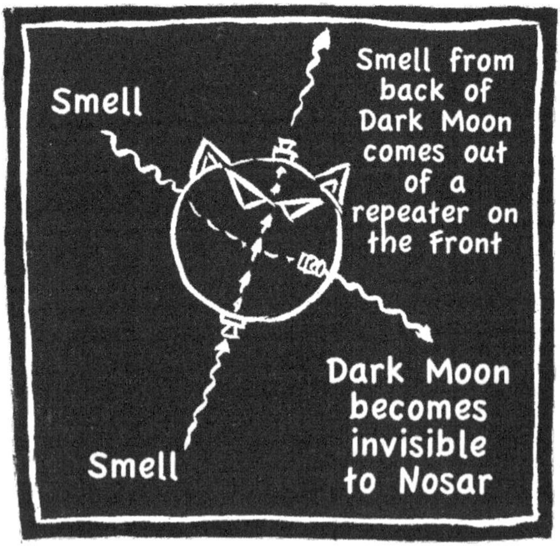

Dark Claw smiled. He liked to show how clever he was. He drew a diagram of how it all worked.

"These repeaters pick up a smell from one side of Dark Moon and send it out again on the other. The smell of Dark Moon stays where it is.

Ratuschka's eyes opened wide. She understood what it meant. "Dark Moon will be invisible to the Muss!" She gasped.

"Precisely!" Dark Claw clapped his paws. "Once we are invisible we can begin the master plan... to put an end to the Muss race forever, and Onlee One in particular."

Dark Claw glowed with pride.

With Dark Claw in such a good mood, Ratuschka dared to ask him something she'd always wanted to know.

"Dark Claw… why do you hate Muss so much?" Straight away she wished she hadn't asked. Dark Claw fixed her with a stare that turned her blood to ice.

"That is my business!" he hissed through clenched teeth.

In the Year Five study at the Tan Monastery School, Hammee was making more toast.

"There's hardly room to butter a sandwich in here," he complained.

"You've won so many trophies and medals, Onlee One, I think it's time you retired!"

Onlee One rolled his eyes. He, Hammee and Chin Chee were prize-winning tunnel-mazers.

As well as trophies, they often won huge pieces of cheese. Cheese was Hammee's favourite food. He couldn't really want Onlee One to retire!

Still, the huge collection of trophies set Onlee One thinking. He looked at his friend Chin Chee.

"Why am I so good at tunnel-mazing and stuff?" he asked. "I don't even have to try hard, it just comes naturally."

Chin Chee smiled. There *was* something special – something different – about Onlee One.

Onlee One was an orphan. He had arrived at the Monastery as a baby, not knowing who his parents were. All he knew was that he had acquired a special gift – an amazing sense of smell! Now, more than ever, Onlee One wanted to know about his past.

As they lined up for supper that night, Onlee One stared at a painting on the wall. It was a portrait of Pale One, the school's most famous former student.

“He’s always been my hero,” said Onlee One. “The trouble is, I’ve broken all the school records that he set. What happens when you are equal with your hero?”

The other two said nothing. It was best to keep quiet when he was in one of these moods.

Onlee One and Pale One shared the same name. But that didn’t have to mean anything … did it?

Onlee One nodded. “I’ve made up my mind,” he said. I’m going to see Abbot Grey after supper. I’m going to ask him who I am!

***

All the Monastery orphans went to Abbot Grey when they were old enough to find out who their parents were. If anyone could tell them, he could.

The kind old Muss smiled at Onlee One. “Yes” he sighed, “it’s time you knew how you came to be given to the Monastery.

Wait here, there's someone I'd like you to meet.

A few minutes later, Abbot Grey returned with the school cook. He put his hands on the cook's shoulders and smiled at Onlee One. This... is your mother!

Onlee One's neck hairs stood on end.
A thrill swept through his body.
His ears twitched out of control.
He couldn't help it.

"Mother!?" Onlee One gasped.

"My little boy!" A tear rolled down the cook's cheek.

Abbot Grey left them alone.

Onlee One's mother smiled shyly. "There must be a million questions you want to ask me?"

Onlee One was lost for words. Looking into her eyes, he suddenly saw his own. The same colour - the same shape. It was true! She really was his mother. He threw himself into her arms and cried like a baby… he couldn't help it!

She held him close for a long time.

Eventually, Onlee One broke the silence. "If you are my mother, who is my father?"

She didn't answer straight away. She stared out of the window, as if she was looking for something… or someone.

Deep in his heart Onlee One knew what she would say. When she finally spoke, her voice was choked with sadness.

"Pale One was your father." She whispered.

"I always knew it," he whispered.

***

Over the next few weeks, Onlee One got to know his mother well. They spent hours looking at old photographs and talking together in her room.

Onlee One pointed to a picture of Pale One.

"What's that mark on his arm?" he asked.

“That’s a long story.” His mother said. “Your father was sent on a mission to the Planet Kat. He became friendly with a Kat family and sometimes stayed at their home.”

“Sadly, he gave their kitten a cold. A cold is not serious for us, but the kitten became very ill. It had to spend the rest of it’s life in a wheelchair.”

“The kitten’s claws were all white, except for one, so they called it ‘Dark Claw.’ Your father had a dark claw tattooed on his arm so that he would never forget.”

Onlee One looked at the scar on his own forearm. It was exactly the same size and shape as his father’s tattoo.

He had been wounded by that same dark claw! Could destiny have bound Onlee One and Dark Claw together so closely?

Onlee One pointed to another picture. It was a picture of Pale One and another Muss. "That looks like Brandling!" he said, in surprise.

"It is," said his mother. "They were best friends at school. It was Brandling who told me that your father had gone missing on an important mission. I was out of my mind with worry."

She blew her nose then carried on with her story. "Your father never returned.

Brandling took me to a nunnery where I hid away for years. The nuns told everyone that my baby had died. They thought it was for the best."

"Eventually, I felt better, and found out that you were alive. I left the nunnery and came here, looking for you. The Abbot was very kind and gave me a job. But he would not let me tell you who I was until you were old enough to accept the truth. It's been very hard to keep the secret."

***

Onlee One wrote to Chancellor Brandling. He asked if it was possible to go to the planet Kat, to find out more about his father. A reply came quickly.

A new ambassador was leaving for Kat very soon. As Onlee One and his friends were such a famous tunnel-mazing team, they could represent the youth of Muss on the mission.

Brandling came to see them off. She was thrilled to learn that Onlee One was her old friend's son.

Before their ship left, she talked about Pale One.

“The nuns told everyone you had died in childbirth,” she explained “Your father took the news very badly. He went to the planet Kat and was never heard of again. I still miss him. He was my best friend.”

“I hope I can learn more about him from the Kats,” said Onlee One. “I may also learn more about Dark Claw too.”

Brandling nodded wisely. “Keep me informed, young One. Send me news of what you find out. We think Dark Claw may be up to his old tricks again.”

“I will,” said Onlee One. “And thank you for making this trip possible.”

Brandling bowed her head slightly. “Anything for the son of my dearest old friend, Pale One.”

***

Everything on the planet Kat was a bit bigger than it was on the planet Muss – because Kats are bigger than Muss!

Onlee One, Hammee and Chin Chee were curious about the strange new planet they were on.

“This stew is an interesting colour,” said Hammee. “What’s in it?”

"Toad Brains!" said their host.

Hammee turned green and felt a little sick.

"Actually," their host said with a smile, "they're not really toad's brains, they just look like them. They're really a sort of apple dumpling."

Hammee sighed with relief. "Mmmmm! Delicious!"

The three friends travelled the planet showing off their amazing tunnel-mazing skills where ever they went.

At the end of the trip they were invited to meet Top Kat at an official dinner. He was the leader of the Kats and a little bit scary.

“So, you are the son of Pale One!” he boomed. “We remember him well.”

“You knew my father?” Onlee One was amazed. I was hoping to find out more about him while I was here.”

The Kat Leader smiled at him. “We knew you were coming so we did some checking. We think he went to the planet Libera with the Purrley family.”

Libera was near the planet Felicity. In the bad old days, the Muss and the Kats had fought over Felicity and destroyed it.

It had been a green and beautiful planet, now it was just a frozen desert. The Kats and Muss were so shocked by what they had done, they made peace with each other and vowed never to go to war with each other again.

Some Kats and Muss had gone to Libera to learn to live together in peace and harmony.

Onlee One felt a question burning inside him. Did the Purrley family have a kitten called Dark Claw?

Top Kat's eyes narrowed. "So you know about him, do you?"

Top Kat took a deep breath. "Dark Claw was a very clever kitten. He built a robo-suit and freed himself from his wheelchair.

Then he built his army of Robo Kats and disappeared with them. He's a very dangerous Kat, but no one knows where he is.

On the journey home, Onlee One went to the control room. He sent a message to Brandling, telling her what he had found out about his father and Dark Claw.

The captain showed him the controls. He was pointing out their position on the Nosar screen when something hit the side of the ship.

"We're under attack!" the pilot shouted.

"We can't be!" The captain pointed at the Nosar screen. "There's nothing there!"

"Kerrang!" something else hit them hard. On the view screen, a Pi-rat ship shot past them, lasers blazing.

"Red alert!" yelled the captain. "Return fire!"

Alarms sounded throughout the ship. Onlee One's heart thumped like a drum. This couldn't be happening. He recognised the Pi-rat ship instantly, he had once captured and flown it himself!

"Ratuschka!" he hissed. "That means Dark Claw can't be too far away!"

The floor shook as their massive laser cannons fired in defence. The Pi-rat ship turned and fled. But where to? It still didn't show up on the Nosar.

If the Pi-rats were invisible maybe Dark Claw was too. Onlee One wasted no time sending a new message to Brandling. The sooner she knew the better.

Their ship was slightly damaged, but they limped home and landed safe and sound.

Hammee was impatient for some "real" home-cooked Muss food again. He licked his lips as the outside doors slid open.

A squad of Muss guards were waiting for them. “Come with us!” ordered the leader.

They were taken to a small room and locked inside. The three friends sat on a bench and waited.

"This feels like a prison cell," said Chin Chee.

"And a prison cell is exactly what it is!" Brandling announced, as she appeared in the doorway. "You are all under arrest!"

The three young Muss couldn't believe their ears. "What?! Why? What for?"

Brandling bared her teeth. It wasn't a smile, more a horrible, cold grimace.

"You will be charged with treason in the morning," she snarled. Then, as quickly as she had come, she was gone.

The door slammed shut behind her.

Invisible to the Muss, Dark Claw watched the latest Seekah spy reports on Dark Moon's control room screens.
He turned to his Pi-rat helpers.

"Well done, Ratushka!" he smirked. "Your little run-in with the Muss has done the trick. My master-plan is working perfectly."

Then Dark Claw whispered quietly to himself. "Revenge will be mine in time... revenge will be mine!"

Breakout!
Book Four

"This is so unfair! We're innocent!" Onlee One shouted. He gritted his teeth in frustration.

The Guards laughed. "Hah! That's what they all say. Don't you worry, there will be plenty of time to complain where you're going!"

Using electric shock-prods, the guards jabbed Onlee One Chin Chee and Hammee. The electric current made the three Muss feel woozy and helpless.

They were thrown on board a prison ship. The door slammed shut behind them and the engines roared into life.

There was only one place they could be going… Pen. The prison planet where all criminal Muss were sent. Onlee One and his friends were desperate. How had they ever got into this awful mess?

Meanwhile, on board his secret space station, Dark Moon, Dark Claw smiled as he watched a video report from one of his Seekahs. The robot Seekahs had planted secret spy cameras all over the Planet Muss.

When the three young Muss had been accused of spying by Chancellor Brandling, Dark Claw had watched their trial with interest. He knew they were innocent and he knew they couldn't prove it. He chuckled as he watched Onlee One and his friends being prodded onto the prison ship.

"At last," hissed Dark Claw. "I have him where I want him." He turned to Ratuschka, leader of the Pi-rat gang that did all his dirty work. He handed her a gold disk.

The disk was Chancellor Brandling's passport that was given to Ratushka in Muss Vegas. The radio signal it gave out, meant she could fly her spaceship unhindered by Muss space patrols.

"This is the key to my plan," Dark Claw chuckled. "You know what to do?"

Ratuschka smiled. She too had a score to settle with Onlee One.

"Oh yes, Dark Claw, you can trust me. I know what to do."

Planet Pen is a drab place. The sky is brown, the ground is brown, and the few bits of trees and grass are brown.

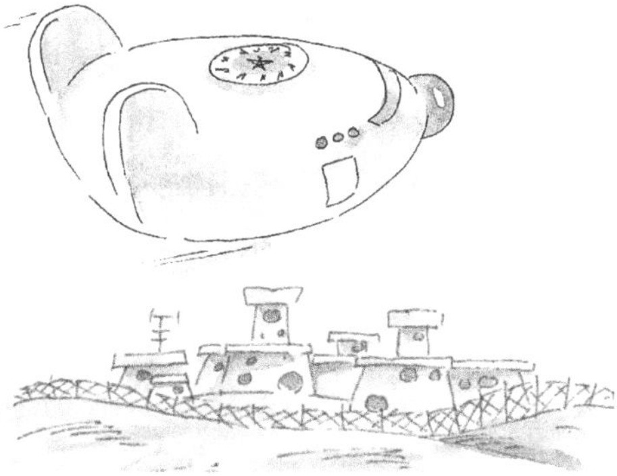

On Pen, the guards - and the spaceport - are locked inside a place called Freetown. A high electric fence surrounds them. All Pen prisoners live outside the fence, locked away from the spaceport, which is the only way to get off the planet.

The prisoners run everything themselves. The guards are only there to stop them from escaping.

Onlee One, Chin Chee and Hammee were marched to the gates of Freetown and pushed into the wild and lonely outside.

A thin, sly-looking Muss lay on the ground near the gate, chewing a piece of dead, brown grass. He opened one eye and glanced at the three new prisoners.

He got to his feet and beckoned for them to follow him. Twenty minutes later, they arrived at a strange makeshift town, where the buildings seemed to be made out of anything that came to hand.

Huts were made from flattened tin cans or cardboard and shacks were made from old prison vans.

Their guide took the three Muss to the largest building, which was made mostly from old packing cases.

Inside, a large ugly-looking Muss sat at one end of the room. Mean-looking Muss hung around him.

"That's Bono," said the guide. "Be nice to him. He's the king round here." Then, with a lazy wave of his paw, the guide slid away and out of the room.

***

"So! Here are the spies!" bellowed Bono

Hammee was just about to protest that they were not spies, that it was all very unfair and that he was very hungry, when he felt a sharp dig in the ribs from Onlee One.

"Quiet! Don't say a word," Onlee One hissed.

Through large, dark glasses, Bono examined the trio one at a time.

"Round here, you do what I tell you." he sneered. "I'm the boss…understand?"

The three friends muttered.

Bono yelled in their faces.

UNDERSTAND?!

"YES, SIR!" they shouted back.

Bono face split into a menacing grin. “There, that’s better. Now it’s time for you to get to work.” He turned to two of his Muss gang and snapped his fingers.

“Take them to the treadmills!”

The treadmills were large metal drums which provided electricity for the prison camp.

As prisoners walked inside them, the gears created power the generators.

It was exhausting. After a week of walking, Onlee One reckoned he must have trodden hundreds of miles. All the walking gave Onlee One time to think - to try and make sense of what had happened to him and his friends.

“Something must have happened a long time ago, between Brandling and my father, Pale One,” he thought. “Now that Brandling knows who I am, she wants me out of the way.”

Round and round went the wheel, day in, day out. As he walked, Onlee One looked at the old wheels and bits of machinery that lay scattered around the treadmills. Slowly an idea floated into his mind.

The treadmills were very like Road Ragers, like the one he had raced on the planet Muss Vegas.

Onlee One took his friends to the dump during their meal break. “Here,” he said, “give us a hand lifting up this old wheel.”

The power gears were broken, but the rest of the wheel was fine. Onlee One got inside and started to rock it back and forth. He soon managed to get the wheel rolling. Holding onto the central axel, he used his feet to keep the wheel turning.

Chin Chee and Hammee ran alongside as the huge wheel picked up speed.

A crowd gathered round to watch. Everyone cheered as the wheel clattered across the ground, a trail of dust flying behind it.

“I’m Road Raging!” Onlee One cheered.

Bono was waiting for him when he returned. His lip curled. He was almost smiling! “This looks fun!” he said. “I’ll find someone to race against you. If you win, I’ll take you off the treadmills.”

“It’s a deal,” Onlee One, panted.

***

Later that day two wheels were made ready for the race. Bono’s rider, Lymee, was big and strong.

"You can beat him," said Chin Chee. "He may be big but you are nimble."

"Please win!" whined Hammee. "I'm fed up with treadmilling!"

The race was hard. Lymee was easing into the lead when some rocket engines roared over their heads.

"Don't look up!" Onlee One told himself.

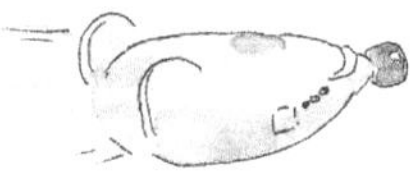

Lymee looked up. He lost his balance for a moment, tripped and was flung around inside the wheel. By the time he'd steadied himself, Onlee One had streaked ahead.

"Concentrate on the race." Onlee One told himself. "It's only a new batch of prisoners being delivered to this terrible planet."

Onlee One was on a roll. He needed to win this race. Lymee was strong and was catching up, but not quickly enough. Onlee One cruised over the winning line, whooping, cheering and punching the air!

For a few minutes he'd forgotten all about his problems. For a few minutes he'd actually been having fun!

Chinchee and Hammee ran towards him, cheering and clapping him on the back. The crowd parted to let Bono through.

"Well done lad!" Bono grinned. "That was good sport. We all need that to keep our spirits up on this forsaken planet. I'll see about finding some easier work for you and your friends."

Hammee and Chin Chee jumped on top of Onlee One. “You were brilliant!” they shouted.

Their cheers were drowned out by a loud siren and a harsh voice hailing them from a hover patrol. “Onlee One, lie down on the ground. Everyone else move away.”

The hover patrol bristled with lasers. Onlee One did as he was told.

A guard leaped out of the patrol and handcuffed him. Before he knew what was happening, Onlee One was in the vehicle and zooming off to Freetown without even a wave goodbye.

***

Onlee One couldn’t believe his eyes. “Chancellor Brandling!” he gasped.

Brandling held her arms out wide.
Onlee One let out a sigh of relief. At last, Brandling had learned the truth and had come to sort everything out.
The nightmare was over.

"Dear boy!" The Chancellor spoke in a cheesy, hollow voice. "There's been an awful mistake. I've come to take you home."

"But what about my friends?" he asked.

"Don't worry," Brandling assured him. "We'll get them out as soon as we can."

Brandling signed a few papers and led Onlee One to the spaceport. She pointed to a boarding ramp.

“After you,” she said. “I’m sure you’re keen to get away from here.”

As Onlee One walked up the ramp, he began to feel uneasy. His sensitive nose smelled Rat! As soon as he entered the spaceship, he recognised it.

He spun round. “This is Ratuschka’s ship!” he gasped. Brandling remained at the bottom of the ramp. From out of the shadows, two large rats grabbed him. The spaceship doors closed. Onlee One could just see Brandling waving.

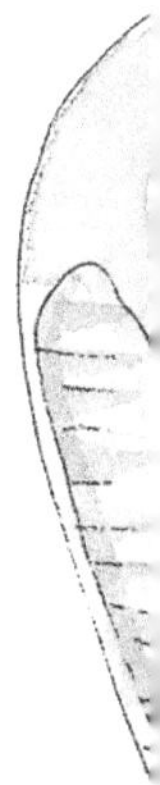

“Bon Voyage, dear boy!” she called.

Onlee One was thrown into a hold and locked in. The engines screamed and wound up to full throttle. They were on their way... but where to?

He looked round his gloomy prison. A faint but familiar smell wafted through the air-vent. He sniffed again.

Onlee One wasn't a Champion Tunnel Mazer for nothing. He soon had the grille off and was squeezing his way through the air system, towards the cockpit.

Ratuschka! There she was, in the cockpit, talking to Dark Claw on a video link.

"We have him, Dark Claw," she announced. "But I'm afraid our price has gone up. If you still want Onlee One, you'll have to pay twice as much as we agreed."

Dark Claw roared with anger. "You have some nerve, Ratuschka. I show no mercy to those who cross me!" He slammed his paw down on the desk in front of him and the screen blanked out.

Ratuschka smiled. "He wants Onlee One more than anything else," she chuckled. "He'll pay up."

Her swarthy crew weren't so sure. They sat in silence, waiting to see what Dark Claw would do. It wasn't long before they found out.

"Now we're for it!" they yelled. "Look at the screen... Robo Kats heading this way. There's hundreds of them! We don't stand a chance!"

Ratuschka shouted over the noise of panic. "We're perfectly safe. Dark Claw wants Onlee One alive!"

But the crew weren't waiting to find out if she was right. They ran to the emergency escape pods. "Let's get out of here! If Dark Claw wants Onlee One, he can have him!"

Airlocks hissed. The escape pods blasted away from the ship

Onlee One was left all alone in the eerie silence. Kicking out the air-vent grille, he lowered himself into the deserted cockpit. The video screen came alive. The image of Dark Claw filled the screen.

"You!" he gasped. "Where is Ratuschka?" Onlee One ignored him as he worked out the ship's controls.

“Where is Ratuschka?” Dark Claw demanded.

Finally, Onlee One looked up at the screen. “She’s gone,” he said calmly. “Just like I’m about to do!”

He eased the control stick forward. The engines roared into life. The power thrust him back into his seat, making it harder for him to set a course. Not that it mattered, any course would do.

“I’m out of here!” he teased the fading image of Dark Claw!

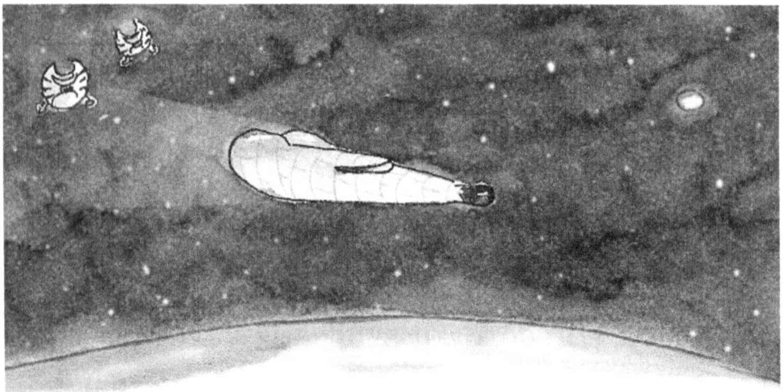

The Robo Kats followed him, but they didn't open fire. "Dark Claw really does want me alive," Onlee One thought.

He checked his position on the star chart and chose a small planet close by to land on. He needed to hide out for a while. Two Robo Kat ships were still on his tail.

Onlee One swept down into the planet's bright pink atmosphere.

He set his ship on autopilot and climbed into the last escape pod.

His spaceship came in low over the purple sea. Onlee One waited until he saw land before pulling the ejector handle.

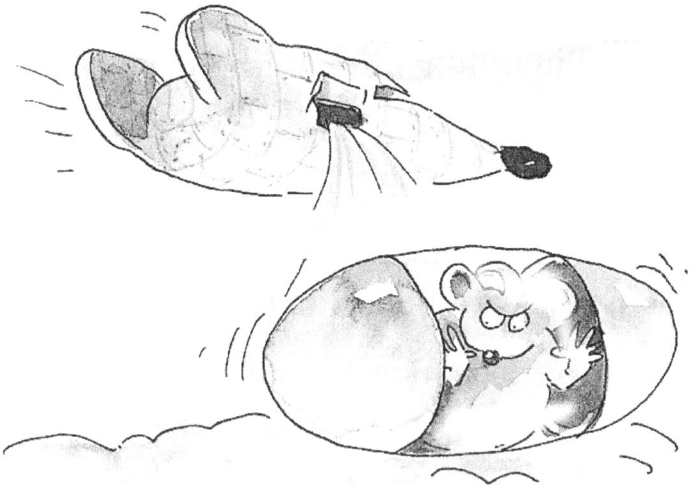

Just before his pod hit the water, Onlee One saw the ship land automatically on the beach. At least he might a way to get back off the planet.

The escape pod crashed into the waves and plunged deep underwater before it slowly rose back to the surface.

Onlee One watched the Robo Kat ships land on the beach next to the Pi-rat ship.

As their sensors showed no life forms in the area, they soon gave up searching for him. With a loud blast of their engines, they headed back to their cruel master.

Onlee One felt very lonely – as though he was the only thing alive on the planet!

"What am I going to do now?" he whispered to himself.

On Dark Moon, the metallic voice of a Robo Kat reported back to Dark Claw.

"All escape pods have been destroyed. Ratuschka and her crew have been dealt with."

The Robokat captain that had chased Onlee One to the planet reported back.

"We have searched the ship. It landed automatically on the planet on Libera. We have been tricked. Onlee One is not on board."

“It cannot be!” Dark Claw roared with rage. “I will have him! I will have my revenge!”

Revenge!

The Guiding Paw
Book Five

"UGH!" Something slimy brushed against Onlee One's paw. Hundreds of putrid, green jellyfish clung to the sides of his escape pod as he paddled to the safety of the beach. A million tiny bubbles fizzed around him. The jellyfish were eating away the metal skin of the escape pod!

Onlee One tried to pick one off but they stung. "Ow!" he squealed.

Onlee One closed his eyes and waited for the end. "After everything I've been through, I'm going to end up being eaten alive by jellyfish!" he sighed.

Meanwhile, across the vast distance of space, Dark Claw paced Dark Moon's control room. Once again, Onlee One had escaped his clutches. Dark Claw raged.

"Onlee One must be destroyed!" he roared. "Onlee One will meet a slow and painful end, I will make sure of it! But first... I must complete my master plan."

With his army of Robo Kats and attack ships, Dark Claw intended to rid the Universe of the entire population of Planet Muss. He turned to the Robo Kat captain.

"We must move quickly." He ordered. "We need more attack ships and we need them now! We cannot lose the element of surprise."

The Robokat's thin metallic voice answered him. "Yes Dark Claw. Your will is our command!"

***

Something massive rumbled behind Onlee One's pod. He turned and stared in horror. A giant, scaly, purple sea-serpent loomed above him. Its fierce jaws were crammed with hundreds of tiny, needle-sharp teeth. The serpent lunged at Onlee One.

"Oh no! I'm going to be snake meat!" he screamed.

The monster crashed down into the water. Onlee One smelled its evil breath and felt the escape pod rise on a tidal wave.

Onlee One opened one eye. He was still alive. The sea monster had simply scooped up a mouthful of jellyfish and eaten them. Now it lunged towards him again, and again.

Each time the monster moved, the waves pushed Onlee One closer to the beach, but his escape pod was sinking.

The pod hit a sand bank. Onlee One didn't hesitate.

He leapt into the water as the pod melted away and disappeared beneath the waves.

The sand was soft underfoot, making it difficult to wade through the water. The jelly fish stung him and his lungs were ready to burst, but he drove himself on through the surf until, at last, he collapsed on the warm, dry sand.

***

Onlee One's Pi-rat spaceship had landed itself gently on the beach. Onlee One took in his surroundings so he could find his way back when it was time to leave.

He hadn't eaten proper food for weeks. He was weak from hunger. He set off looking for fresh fruit to eat.

Five minutes later, he came across two deeply-carved stones that stood like gateposts in the sand. The stones marked the entrance to a path that led deep into the jungle.

Onlee One's whiskers twitched. Maybe he wasn't alone on this planet.

He followed the path until it opened out into a mossy glade. A tree stood in the middle, shimmering in a multitude of colours. Warily, Onlee One crossed the glade for a closer look.

"Ribbons!" he whispered in surprise. The tree was covered in them. "I am definitely not alone!" he thought.

Two more gate stones stood at the entrance to a strange building made from huge rocks. The roof was covered in grass. All was silent. Onlee One crept inside.

A dark corridor led him to a circular room. It felt like a chapel or a church. Daylight filtered down from the roof. A Kat's paw was carved above the altar. He'd seen the sign before, on the planet Kat. It was the symbol of The Guiding Paw, the religion of the Kats.

As he turned to go, his heart thumped to a stop.

Twelve tall creatures in long, red, hooded robes, watched him from the shadows. Their yellow eyes glowed beneath their hoods. He couldn't see their faces, but he knew they were Kats.

"Hi!" he said, cheerfully. "Nice place you've got here." If he was nice to them, maybe they wouldn't make a burned sacrifice of him … just yet!

The Kats led Onlee One through the jungle. Ribbons tied to the branches of trees marked their route. Nobody spoke. The jungle suddenly came to an end.

Onlee One squeaked in amazement.

A cliff soared high above them. A Kat town, had been carved from the rock, but there were Muss-holes too.

They made their way up a sweeping staircase to the town gate. A tall white Kat in a gorgeous red robe waited for them.

She spoke gently. “Welcome to Libera. Have no fear. Here, Kat and Muss live together in peace.”

Her name was Spyra. She was the chosen leader. She told him how the Kats and Muss had once fought each other and destroyed the beautiful planet of Felicity.

“Some of us Kats and Muss were so shocked by what we had done,” she explained. “We decided to come to Libera, and learn to live together.”

Food and drink were brought for Onlee One and he began to tell his story.

When he mentioned Dark Claw, Spyra’s face clouded over.

"The Dark Claw you speak of is my son," she sighed. It was hard to believe that this beautiful, gentle creature could be the mother of anything as evil as Dark Claw.

Onlee One held her gaze. "If Dark Claw is your son, then you once knew my father, Pale One."

Her eyes narrowed as she examined his features. Then she nodded as she saw the likeness in his face. She lifted her paw, signalling to the crowd of Kats and Muss behind her

There was a movement and an older Muss, that had been standing in the shadows, came to her side.

"I am Pale One!" he said.

Onlee One's eyes nearly popped!

***

"Brandling!" sighed Pale One. "It was Brandling that told me you and your Mother had died. After that, there was nothing left for me to do on Muss." Onlee One had told his story. Now it was his father's turn.

"When Dark Claw was a kitten, he caught a bad cold from me." Pale One explained, "He was so ill that he became unable to walk and needed a wheelchair."

Pale One gazed at his son. "I thought you were dead. I went back to help bring up Dark Claw. I suppose I felt guilty. It was my fault that he had been so ill."

Pale One looked sad. The memories came flooding back to him.

"Dark Claw was always angry," he explained. "We thought it was because he couldn't walk. But perhaps he was just plain bad through and through?"

"He was very clever. He made his own Robo-suit that allowed him to walk."

"After his father died in a tragic accident, Dark Claw disappeared. Spyra came here and I came with her."

Onlee One listened to his father intently. He felt he had known him all his life. "Will you come and help us fight Dark Claw, Father?"

Pale One smiled. "I never thought I'd hear myself called Father." He pulled Onlee One to him and hugged him tight.

"I have vowed to work for peace," Pale One told his son. "This is your fight - it is up to you now.
May the
Guiding Paw
be with you."

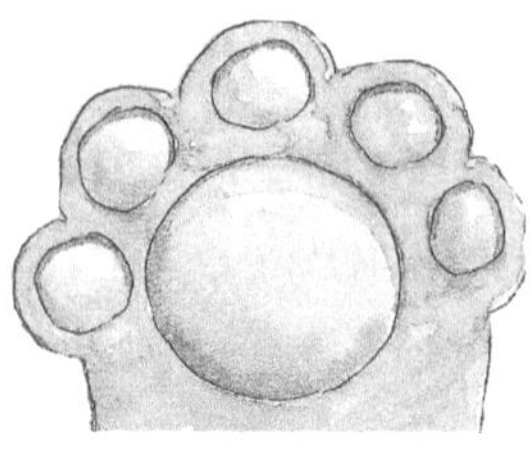

Onlee One's spacecraft sped across the Universe. He was returning to rescue his friends from the prison planet, Pen. A few kind Kats and Muss had helped him clean up the ship and load it with stores. He looked out of the control room window. There was something out there.

It was Dark Moon!

It was surrounded by a huge fleet of Robo Kat ships… hundreds of them! Onlee One filmed them on a vid-cam and then filmed the Nosar screen.

"None of these ships show up on the screen," he explained on the camera. "Dark Claw has found a way to be invisible to Muss Nosar!"

He quickly altered course before he was spotted and attacked. It wasn't long before Pen came into sight.

Onlee One slipped the gold disk passport that Brandling had given to Ratuschka, into the control panel. It allowed him to land on Pen without trouble.

Onlee One flew right down to the planet's surface, to where he knew his friends Hammee and Chin Chee would be.

The ship hovered by the treadmills. Onlee One's voice boomed over the loudspeakers. "No one move! Hammee and Chin Chee walk towards the ship, now."

As his two old friends recognised the ship, huge grins broke out on their faces. They ran as fast as their tired legs would let them. Onlee One hardly recognised Hammee. He'd lost so much weight!

Hammee and Chin Chee climbed on board and were reunited with their old friend in the control room.

Tears filled Hammee's eyes as he hugged Onlee One.

"I don't suppose there's anything to eat?" He asked in weak, pathetic, voice! "I am so-o-o hungry!"

***

“Pooh! Disgusting!” said Hammee. The three friends were in a sewer underneath the President’s palace. The passport had allowed the trio to land close to the palace. The sewers were the only way in.

Onlee One climbed a ladder, gently lifted a Muss-hole cover a crack, and peered into a courtyard. “We’re inside the palace!”

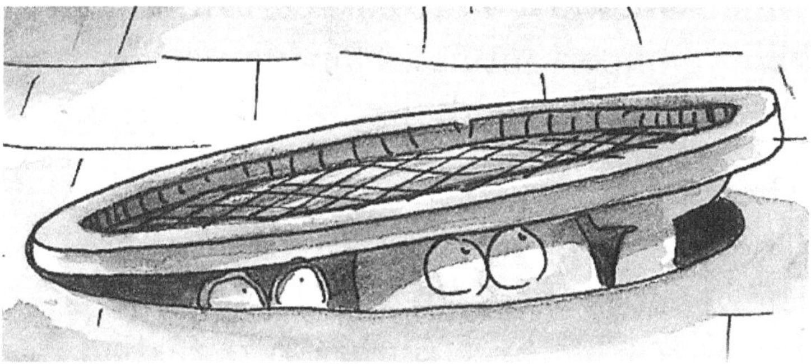

They climbed out of the hole, quietly replaced the lid, and ran to the shadows. Onlee One had met Top Muss before. With his incredible sense of smell, he now detected a tiny scent of the chief Muss and followed his phenomenal nose.

The three friends crept through corridors and tiptoed down passages. “He’s behind that door,” whispered Onlee One.

Onlee One sniffed again and looked alarmed! "So is Brandling!"

"What about the guards?" hissed Chin Chee.

Onlee One took out Brandling's passport. "Let's try this."

Boldly, they walked toward the guards. Onlee One waved the passport in the air. "We've important news for Chancellor Brandling," he said, firmly.

The guards looked unsure, but as Onlee One was carrying Brandling's passport, they opened the doors and let them through. The three young Muss rushed into the presidential office.

Brandling and the President were examining some papers. Brandling's jaw dropped when she saw who had just burst into the room.

Onlee One spoke. "Your honour, our planet is in great danger. Dark Claw is building a huge army that cannot be detected by Nosar." Onlee One held up the vid-cam.

“I have proof.”

Brandling laughed. “What nonsense! Who ever heard of such a thing? Guards! Arrest these fools!”

Onlee One held up the golden passport disk. “I also have proof of Chancellor Brandling’s treachery!”

Top Muss held up a paw to stop the guards. He spoke with great authority. “I think we should see the evidence before we make up our minds.”

Brandling smiled nervously. “Of course,

your honour!"

They watched the video in silence. When it was finished, Top Muss was ashen-faced. He stayed silent for a

moment, deep in thought, before he spoke.

"Well, what do you have to say for yourself, Brandling?!"

But Brandling had gone! She had slipped out of a side door while they were watching the video.

Onlee One told Top Muss how Brandling had imprisoned them and was working in league with Dark Claw.

"I have often doubted Brandling's loyalty," said Top Muss. "Never have the Muss faced such a fearful enemy as Dark Claw. He has grown strong thanks to Brandling's treachery."

Top Muss put an arm on Onlee One's shoulder. "You have done well, young Onlee One. Let us hope you are not too late!"

Top Muss called out to the guards, "Search the palace. Arrest Brandling. She must not escape!"

***

Meanwhile on Dark Moon, Dark Claw was lost in thought. His robot Seekahs had sent him news of Onlee One's escape.

"There is no time to lose," he growled. "We must get ready for the attack on Muss, before we lose the element of surprise. He pushed a button that sent a signal to the whole Robo Kat fleet...

"Code Red: Prepare for invasion!"

Dark Claw watched as his vast armada of spaceships get themselves battle ready.

"Revenge will be mine." He purred.

Revenge will be mine!

The Black Hole
Book Six

"Halt, or be destroyed!" A Robo Kat's voice crackled over the radio. Chancellor Brandling slammed on the reverse thrusters.

"This is Chancellor Brandling from the Planet Muss. I request an urgent meeting with Dark Claw."

"Wait there!" came the Robo Kat's reply.

The Chancellor sat fuming in her spacecraft. Onlee One had escaped death once again and spoiled her plan to be ruler of all Muss! Now she could never go home again, unless... maybe she could strike a deal with Dark Claw?

The Rob Kat's thin, reedy voice broke into her thoughts. "Dark Claw will speak with you… proceed."

Brandling smiled to herself. Now Dark Claw had agreed to meet with her, he was bound to agree to her plan! The hardest part of her mission was over. She slid the control stick forward and set a course for Dark Moon.

Top Muss was meeting with the Grand Muss Council. Before him stood a group of nervous guards and officials.

All of them had worked for Brandling. Now that she had deserted them, they were certain they would be charged with treason, just as Brandling had been.

Top Muss addressed them. "Dark Claw is our most deadly enemy and Brandling is now in league with him. She cannot save you now. If you'll work with us to save the planet Muss from Dark Claw, you will be forgiven the error of your ways."

The traitors had expected to go to prison at the very least. They did not hesitate. "We promise!" they cried.

“Long live Top Muss! Long live the Planet!”

Top Muss looked across at Onlee One and his two friends, Hammee and Chin Chee. His mood stayed serious. “Once again, Onlee One has saved the planet from certain danger. He and his team have risked their lives to help save our planet. We owe him our undying thanks.”

The Council members nodded in agreement.

"But we are not out of danger yet!" Top Muss continued. "We must rid the Universe of Dark Claw, for ever!"

He swept out of the Council Chamber, beckoning all to join him in the planning room. "Come! There is very little time!"

Brandling's guards and officials followed quickly. Brandling was just a memory. Now there was serious work to be done!

On Dark Claw's secret space station, Dark Moon, Brandling was explained her plan.

"I understand your hatred of Onlee One, Dark Claw, but there is no need to destroy us all."

Dark Claw's cold expression did not alter.

"Why destroy all Muss?" Brandling questioned. "Let them be your slaves. I will help you take command of the Muss. They respect me."

Feeling more confident, Brandling continued. "When I give the order, my trusted servants will overthrow Top Muss. I will become their new leader, and you will become Master of the Universe!"

Brandling let the idea sink in. Dark Claw looked thoughtful.

"What about Onlee One?" he growled.

"Onlee One?" exclaimed Brandling. "Oh, I have big plans for him. He'll wish he'd never been born!"

"Excellent!" said Dark Claw. "I have plans for him, too. Perhaps we can make him suffer twice?"

"Ha! Ha! Ha!" Brandling, laughed nervously. She'd rather not know what Dark Claw had in mind for any Muss that crossed him.

“Very well,” said Dark Claw. “Give your orders and commands, but never forget that I am your Master!” He pressed a button on the control panel and spoke into the console microphone.

“Let the invasion begin!” he hissed.

A Robo Kat's voice answered. "Yes, Dark Claw. All space craft go to code green. Begin the invasion!"

Dark Claw and Brandling watched from the control room window and as the massive fleet set course for planet Muss.

Dark Claw spoke just loud enough for Brandling to hear. "I do not forgive failure."

***

Brandling's old secretary, Ruse, approached Top Muss with his head bowed. "I've had a message from Brandling," he said. "She's ordered me to have you locked up. Then she will return as our new leader."

Top Muss looked Ruse straight in the eye. "And are you going to follow her orders?" he asked.

"O-o-f course n-n-not," stammered Ruse

"Good!" Top Muss smiled. "Now, tell us about Brandling's plan."

A huge map was covered in images of Muss spaceships, but there was no sign of Dark Claw's fleet. Ruse explained to Top Muss how the Roboships were invisible to Muss Nosar systems.

"The Roboships have smell repeaters on them that move the smell from behind them to in front of them. So our Nosars can't detect the Roboship fleet that is heading towards us.

Top Muss stared at the map. “Where do we think Dark Claw is coming from?” he asked.

Chin Chee pointed to the map with a stick. “Brandling went in this direction, so we think that’s where Dark Claw’s attack will mostly likely come from.”

“Good,” Top Muss nodded, wisely. “Send scout ships in that direction. We must find Dark Claw’s fleet.”

Onlee One looked at Hammee and Chin Chee.

“Come on,” he said. “That means Us!”

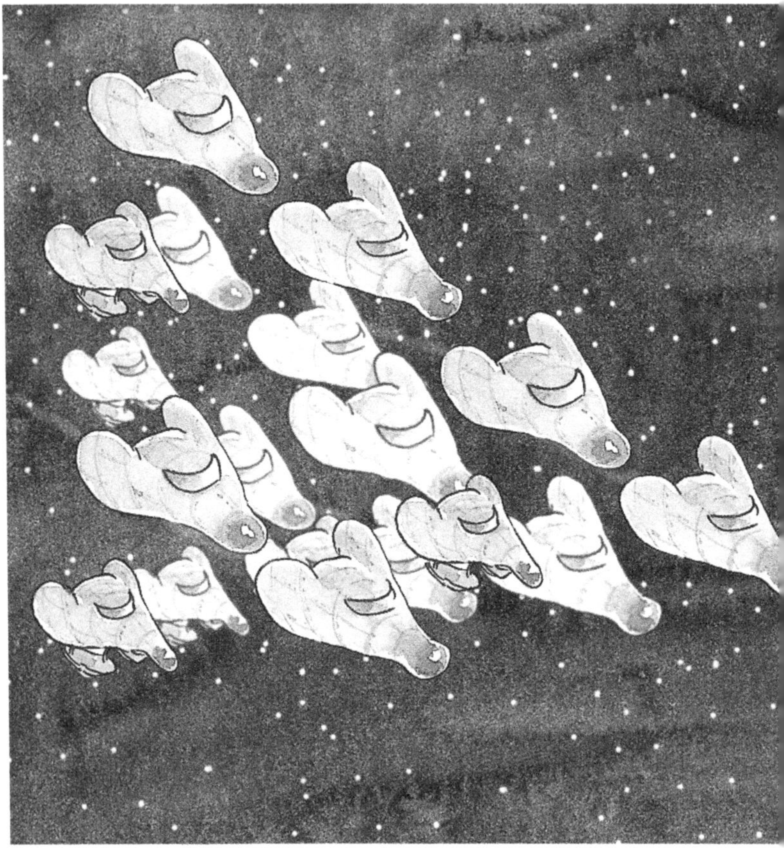

"Great balls of Cheddar Cheese!" The voice of a Star Pilot spilled across the radio. Another voice giggled.

"Language, please!" Onlee One spoke into his headset. "Have you anything to report?" He asked the scout pilots.

The Starpilot's excited voice crackled on the speakers. "I'm at position 29-34-52. It's incredible. There are hundred's... no! ... thousands of Roboships. I can see them but none of them show up on my Nosar.

"Good work!" Onlee One praised. "Now get out of there!"

A moment later the panicked Starpilot came back on air. "I'm under attack! They're..." The radio crackled, then cut out. Every pilot listening breathed a sigh of relief that it had not been them.

Onlee One stayed calm. "Let's look at the starmap." Chin Chee pointed out where Dark Claw's fleet should be. All three of them stared at the screen, trying to work out a plan. It looked hopeless.

Onlee One pointed to some dots on the screen that were heading towards Litterbox, the dirty brown moon that circled the Planet Muss. "What are those ships over there?" He asked.

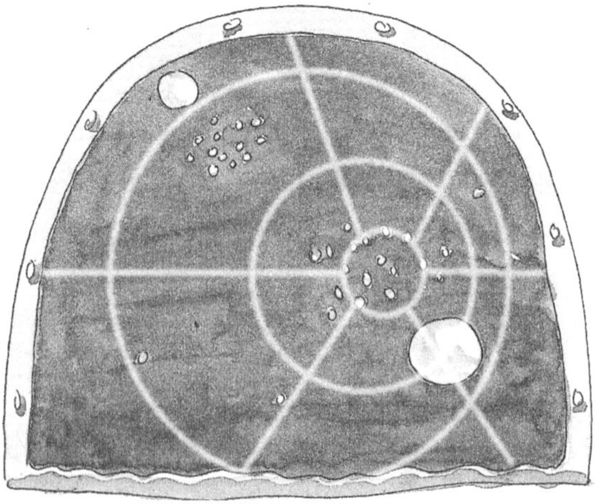

Chin Chee checked their code numbers. "They're just trash barges."

Onlee One looked surprised. "Trash Barges!" he asked. "What do they do?"

They transport all the waste from the Planet Muss to Litterbox," Chin Chee explained. "The waste is mushed up into a liquid and sprayed, so the barges don't have to land on the revolting surface of Litterbox

Onlee One smiled as a tiny idea flickered in his brain, and quickly developed into a plan.

“Right!” he ordered. “Send the barges towards Dark Claw’s fleet and spray them with trash. Then our Nosars will be able to smell them.”

“That is such a crazy idea...” said Hammee “It just might work!”

***

The trash barges were set on course. As they closed in on their target, millions of tons of toxic gloop was sprayed towards Dark Claw’s Armada.

The radios in a thousand Muss fighter craft sprang to life with chattering pilots.

“I’ve got them on the Nosar,” said one. They’re showing up like Candle-trees. We can’t miss them!

The Muss-guided missiles worked on smell, the same way Nosar did. Once they were locked onto that deep space stink, nothing could stop them reaching their targets.

There was no escape for the Robo Kat ships. One by one, as the missiles hit their gloop-covered targets, they exploded into wildly coloured fireballs.

Dark Claw's fisted paw slammed on the control panel. Slowly, he turned his burning yellow eyes towards Brandling. "You have failed me!" he snarled."

"It's not my fault!" Brandling complained. "I've been betrayed as well!"

They were racing back to the safety of Dark Moon. Dark Claw had watched his fleet explode around him. Now he ordered his surviving Roboships to retreat before they too were destroyed.

Onlee One and the other Muss starpilots were hard on their tail.

"It's all Onlee One's fault!" Brandling whimpered.

Dark Claw froze at the sound of his arch enemy's name. Brandling's blood ran cold. She had made a dreadful error!

Dark Claw thrust his paw in front of Brandling's face. His one, dark claw sprung out like a switchblade.

At the signal, two Robo Kat guards leapt forward and grabbed Brandling's arms. Dark Claw prodded Brandling's shoulder.

"No one fails me!" he hissed through gritted teeth. "No one!"

Dark Claw's ship entered the huge landing bay on Dark Moon. The giant space doors began closing behind it.

The Robo Kats marched Brandling to the air-lock door and waited until it was safe to leave the spaceship.

Brandling knew that Dark Claw meant to put her to a slow, painful death, but she decided it would be better to die quickly and painlessly.

She lunged towards the airlock and grabbed the handle. The Robo Kats weren't fast enough to stop her.

With a rising sense of panic, she hurriedly twisted the handle this way and that, until it clicked into the open position.

The air filled with a piercing screech as the door seals broke. The screech turned into a roar as air rushed out of the ship.

The vacuum of space clawed hungrily at the air lock door.

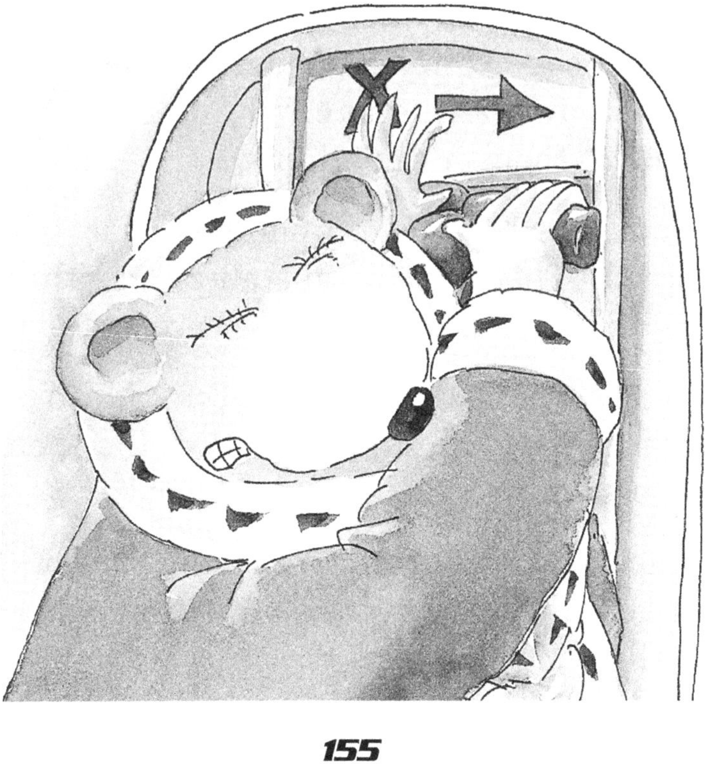

As Brandling felt the air being sucked from her lungs she managed one last laugh. She had beaten Dark Claw.

The door seal snapped against the immense pressure. The door smashed open and every last gasp of air blasted out of the ship and was lost into space.

***

Onlee One, Chin Chee and Hammee circled Dark Moon. Nothing happened. They knew Dark Claw was in there. Why didn't he shoot at them or something?

Chin Chee called over from the Nosar screen. "There's an alien craft coming this way. They say they come in peace."

A strange ship cruised up to Dark Moon's landing bay, and slipped through the open airlock that gaped like a dead fish.

Onlee One felt the fur rise on the back of his neck. "Come on!" he said. "We're going in there too."

A minute later, they landed in the hanger bay, put on their space suits and walked down the ramp, to meet the crew of the alien ship.

Two strangers walked across the hangar bay floor. The smaller one smiled at Onlee One. “You’ve done well, son.”

Onlee One turned to his friends. “This is my father, Pale One. And this is Spyra,” he explained, pointing to the tall, beautiful Kat. “Dark Claw is her son.”

Hammee and Chin Chee, were speechless.

Spyra voice sounded sad. "We have both come to see our children," she sighed.

They followed her into Dark Claw's ship. Brandling's body lay by the door, still holding the airlock handle.

"For once she did the right thing," Pale One said. "She sacrificed herself to save us all."

They found Dark Claw's body in the control room. His one dark claw still pointed from his velveted paw.

The two bodies were wrapped in cloth of gold and thrust out into the vast darkness of space. Silently, side by side, their lifeless bodies sped towards the great Black Hole.

The war was over! On Planet Muss the celebrations lasted for days! Top Muss gave Hammee, Chin Chee and Onlee One the planet's highest honour for bravery. Hammee ate and ate until he was his normal, cuddly self again!

Then came the day for Spyra and Pale One to return home.

"Look after Onlee One for me." Pale One asked Chin Chee.

Chin Chee smiled. "I will."

Onlee One didn't know what to say to Spyra. After all, she had lost her only child in Dark Claw. But Spyra looked deep into his eyes and somehow he knew that words were not needed. She held him close and whispered.

Across the vast eternity of space,
the bodies of Dark Claw and Brandling
entered the singularity of the
Great Black Hole,
where the laws of nature
and the Universe are written
and rewritten in the
twinkling of an eye...

The end?

**Learn more about Dark Claw,
and how to draw him,
the spaceships and other
characters from the book.**

**Find out about other great
books too at Shoo Rayner,s
amazing, Intergalactic Website**

www.shoorayner.com

Dark Claw was originally published as a set of six individual books. This edition contains all six stories bound together for the first time.

The stories have been very slightly revised to make them flow more smoothly.

Not all the original illustrations are included and some of them too, have been edited or revised.

Lightning Source UK Ltd.
Milton Keynes UK
UKOW06f0249090216
268000UK00001B/17/P

9 781908 944177